QUIET PLEASE, OWEN McPHEE!

TRUDY LUDWIG

illustrated by PATRICE BARTON

Alfred A. Knopf New York

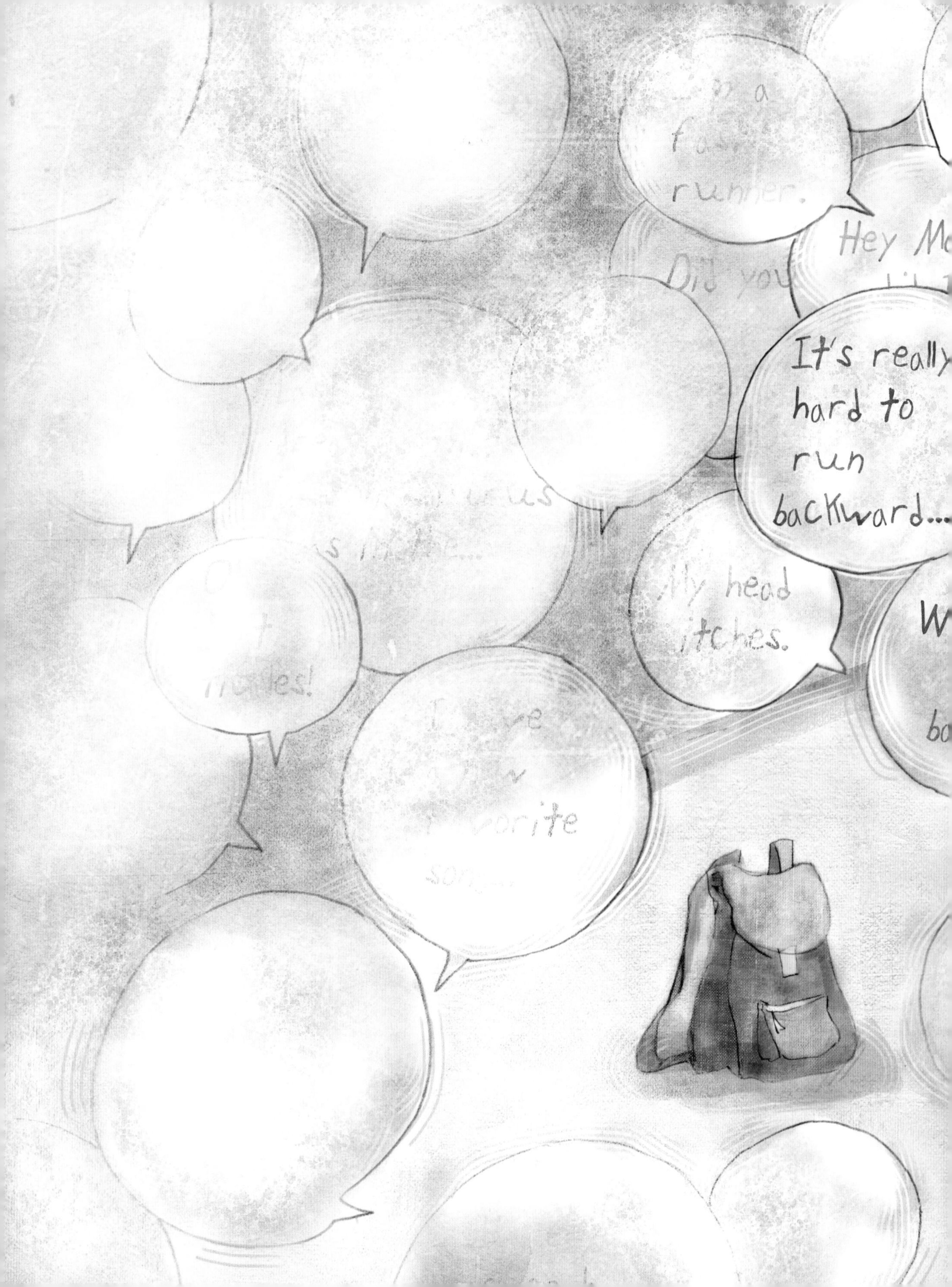
It's really hard to run backward....
My head itches.

Owen McPhee doesn't just like to talk.
He *loves* to talk, morning, noon, and night.
Even Hannah, his loyal hound dog, gets more
than an earful of what Owen has to say.

But sometimes, all that talking can get in the way of listening.

MONDAY

"Remember, scientists," says Mr. Delgado to the students. "When it's your turn to make an erupting volcano, do not—I repeat, DO NOT—put more than one-half cup of baking soda in the—"

My dog, Hannah, can smell 100,000 times better than humans. How cool is that?! Hey, Marcus—do you think your cat smells better than you? Not that YOU smell or anything.

Hahaha...

TUESDAY

WEDNESDAY

"You know what, Owen?" says Marcus as he puts away his tray. "You talk *way* too much!"

But instead of slowing down, they start speeding up.

THURSDAY

In the morning, at the McPhees' breakfast table, something strange happens: Not a single word is heard from Owen! He has a bad case of laryngitis.

With extra paper and pencils in hand, Owen goes to school, determined to write all he won't be able to say.

It doesn't take long, though, for Owen to learn that he can't write as fast as he can talk . . .

. . . or as much as the other kids can talk.

Tired of trying to be heard, Owen heads
back to the classroom.

"I know," she says. "It wasn't going to be strong enough, anyway. I have an idea to make it better, though," she adds. "Would you . . . could you . . . help me?"

Owen smiles as he nods yes.

FRIDAY

There are still times when Owen has
an awful lot to say . . .

. . . but there are also times when he doesn't.

And that's just how Owen likes it.

SUNDAY   M

La
D

7

Ryan's
Birthday
Party   14

2

Laryngit
Day

QUESTIONS FOR DISCUSSION

But, sometimes, all that talking can get in the way of listening.

- In what ways does Owen's nonstop chatter cause problems at school? Give three examples.

- How do the other characters in the story react to Owen's constant talking? Refer to the illustrations and text for clues.

- Do you think it's possible to both talk and listen well at the same time? Why or why not?

"Hey, guys—wait for me!" But instead of slowing down, they start speeding up.

- Why do Marcus and his friends walk away more quickly from the lunch table when Owen asks them to wait for him?

- Is this a case of Owen talking too much or sharing too much information? Explain the difference.

- Has someone ever interrupted you in the middle of a conversation with someone else and then taken over the conversation? If yes, how did that make you feel?

It doesn't take long, though, for Owen to learn that he can't write as fast as he can talk . . . or as much as the other kids can talk.

- How do you think it might feel for someone who is really excited to share their thoughts and experiences not to get a turn to talk?

- Who in the story is able to express herself with the help and support of a quieter Owen?

- Which is harder for you to do—share your ideas and stories with others or be a good listener? Explain why.

There are still times when Owen has an awful lot to say . . . but there are also times when he doesn't. And that's just how Owen likes it.

- Why do you think some kids like to talk a lot and others prefer to listen more than talk?

- When are the best times for talking? For listening? Give three examples of each from your own experience.

- Why is being a good listener such an important and helpful skill in life?

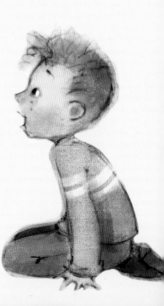

For Charlie, my wonderfully chatty muse at Tuscan Elementary, and
Sherri Roth, a longtime friend and fan from my early storytelling days.
¡Con abrazos! —T.J.L.

To my favorite chatty engineer, Mac —P.B.

"We have two ears and one mouth so that we can listen twice as much as we speak."
—Epictetus

Text copyright © 2018 by Trudy Ludwig

Jacket art and interior illustrations copyright © 2018 by Patrice Barton

All rights reserved. Published in the United States by Alfred A. Knopf, an imprint of Random House Children's Books,

a division of Penguin Random House LLC, New York.

Knopf, Borzoi Books, and the colophon are registered trademarks of Penguin Random House LLC.

Visit us on the Web! rhcbooks.com

Educators and librarians, for a variety of teaching tools, visit us at RHTeachersLibrarians.com

Library of Congress Cataloging-in-Publication is available upon request.

ISBN 978-0-399-55713-2 (trade) — ISBN 978-0-399-55714-9 (lib. bdg.) — ISBN 978-0-399-55715-6 (ebook)

The illustrations in this book were created using pencil sketches digitally painted.

MANUFACTURED IN CHINA

August 2018   10 9 8 7 6 5 4 3 2 1   First Edition

Random House Children's Books supports the First Amendment and celebrates the right to read.